"I'm not an ordinary boy."

"I'm almost a genius," Houdini told M. T. Randal. "I'm a magician, too."

He put his hand near my ear and a penny fell out.

Then he made a fist with his other hand. He dropped the penny in. When he opened his fist, the penny was gone.

M. T. Randal looked at me.

"I'm not a genius or a magician," I told him. "I'm just an ordinary girl."

First Stepping Stone Books you will enjoy:

By David A. Adler
(The Houdini Club Magic Mystery series)
Onion Sundaes

By Mary Pope Osborne
(The Magic Tree House series)
Dinosaurs Before Dark (#1)
The Knight at Dawn (#2)
Mummies in the Morning (#3)
Pirates Past Noon (#4)

By Barbara Park
Junie B. Jones and the Stupid Smelly Bus
Junie B. Jones and a Little Monkey Business
Junie B. Jones and Her Big Fat Mouth
Junie B. Jones and Some Sneaky Peeky Spying

By Louis Sachar
Marvin Redpost: Kidnapped at Birth?
Marvin Redpost: Why Pick on Me?
Marvin Redpost: Is He a Girl?
Marvin Redpost: Alone in His Teacher's House

By Marjorie Weinman Sharmat
The Great Genghis Khan Look-Alike Contest
Genghis Khan: A Dog Star Is Born

A Houdini Club Magic Mystery

Onion Sundaes

by David A. Adler

illustrated by Heather Harms Maione

A FIRST STEPPING STONE BOOK

Random House New York

To Michael, Eddie, and Eitan

 Published in the United States by Random House, Inc., New York, and simultaneously in Canada by Random House of Canada Limited, Toronto.

Library of Congress Cataloging-in-Publication Data
Adler, David A. Onion sundaes / by David A. Adler ; illustrated by Heather Harms Maione.
p. cm. — (A Houdini Club magic mystery ; 1)
"A First Stepping Stone book."
SUMMARY: Aspiring magician Herman "Houdini" Foster and his cousin Janet help uncover the thief who is stealing money from shoppers at the supermarket.
ISBN 0-679-84697-2 (trade) — ISBN 0-679-94697-7 (lib. bdg.)
[1. Stealing—Fiction. 2. Magic tricks—Fiction. 3. Supermarkets—Fiction. 4. Mystery and detective stories.] I. Maione, Heather Harms, ill. II. Title. III. Series: Adler, David A. Houdini Club magic mystery ; 1.
PZ7.A26150n 1994 [E]—dc20 93-5878
Manufactured in the United States of America
10 9 8 7 6 5 4 3 2 1

Random House, Inc. New York, Toronto, London, Sydney, Auckland

1

Onion Magic

I watched Houdini Foster.

He was wearing his black cape. He held out his arms, bowed, and smiled real big. He was about to do a magic trick.

"Good afternoon, ladies and gentlemen," he said. "I, the Great Houdini, am about to mystify and amaze you."

Houdini sat down at the table in his kitchen. In front of him was a dish of vanilla ice cream, a spoon, a red paper tube, and an onion.

Houdini had set six chairs in a row. I

was sitting in one. The other five were empty. But Houdini was pretending there was someone in each chair.

Houdini said, "And now, ladies and gentlemen, my cousin Janet Perry is about to eat an onion sundae."

"I'm not eating anything that has onions in it or near it," I told Houdini. "Onions and I just don't get along!"

Houdini smiled at the empty chairs. Then he whispered to me, "Please, there are people watching."

"I'm not eating onions," I told him again. "And that's final!"

Houdini smiled again. This time I could see some of his back teeth.

Houdini picked up the red tube. He held it up for every chair to see.

"My cousin says she doesn't like onions," he said. "I guess I'll have to change this onion into something she does like."

Houdini picked up the onion. "Now watch me. Watch me very carefully," he said.

He raised his right eyebrow. Then he raised his left eyebrow. He can do that. He's very talented.

Houdini has deep dark brown eyes. I do, too. Our mothers are sisters, and in some ways we look alike.

Houdini dropped the onion into the top of the red paper tube.

He waved his magic wand and said, "*Ala-kazam,* I am great. Yes, I am."

Those are his magic words.

Then he picked up the tube. There on the table was what looked like a jar of chocolate syrup!

I opened the jar and dipped my finger

into the syrup. It tasted like chocolate.

Houdini smiled. He showed me the red tube. I looked right through it. There was nothing inside.

"How did you do that?" I asked.

Houdini stood up and bowed to the chairs. This time he gave the chairs his *real* big smile. I think I saw a cavity in one of his back teeth.

"I watched you very carefully and I still don't know how you did it," I said.

"When I did the magic trick, you were watching the wrong thing," Houdini said. "You were looking at me. Never watch the magician. Watch his props."

Houdini waved good-bye to the empty chairs.

"The audience is leaving now," he told me. "But they'll be back. They liked my Onion Sundae Trick."

Houdini bowed again.

Then he said to me, "I'll teach you the trick. I'm really nice that way. I'm willing to give you the benefit of my great mind."

That's how Houdini talks. He tells me lots of times how great he is. But I don't mind. He's fun.

Houdini is almost a genius. I'm not. I'm good at math and I like spiders and I can wiggle my left ear. But except for that, I'm just like any other nine-year-old girl.

Houdini said, "I'll teach the trick to everyone at our Houdini Club meeting this afternoon."

He picked up the dish of ice cream. "Let's put this away before it melts," he said.

"Don't put it away!" I told him. "I want to eat my chocolate sundae."

"We'll buy ice cream for the club and eat it at the meeting," he told me.

I waved good-bye to the ice cream as

Houdini put it away. He washed the dishes and put the chairs back. I licked the ice cream scoop, and then I washed it.

Houdini said, "I have the paper and rubber bands to make the tubes. But I'll need plastic spoons and bowls. I'll also need lots of ice cream. And onions."

Houdini packed his backpack with the paper, rubber bands, and his magic wand and black cape. He also took along his "Magic Money" wallet. That's where he keeps the money he earns for performing at kids' parties. He uses the money to buy things for his magic tricks.

I made a list of everything we would need. Onions. Ice cream. Spoons. Bowls.

"We can get everything at the Super Big 'N' Super Friendly Supermarket," Houdini said. "Let's go."

2

My Money Is Gone!

Houdini's real name is Herman Foster. But he doesn't like to be called Herman. He says Herman is too ordinary a name for him.

Last year he read a book about Harry Houdini, the world's greatest magician. Then Herman began practicing magic tricks. And he began calling *himself* Houdini. Now everyone calls him that.

A few months ago Herman "Houdini" Foster started the Houdini Club. We meet in our friend Dana's basement. Mostly, we watch Houdini do magic tricks. Usually, after he does a trick, he shows us how he did it.

As we walked toward the supermarket, Houdini talked about one of his favorite subjects. The Great Harry Houdini.

"The real Houdini was the world's greatest escape artist. In 1899 he told the police to lock him up in metal chains. He hadn't done anything wrong. He just wanted to prove that he could get out. And he did—in less than one minute!

"I'm studying locks and escapes," my cousin Houdini told me. "Right now I can get into a locked bathroom."

That's easy. Even I can do that. All I need is a hair clip.

Once I walked in on my mother. She was only brushing her teeth. But she got angry anyway. She said she *could* have been doing something else.

We were waiting at the corner for the traffic light to change.

Houdini told me, "The Great Harry Houdini once led an elephant onto a stage and into a large wooden box. There was no place for the elephant to go. But when the box was opened, the elephant was gone."

The traffic light changed.

"I'd like to try that trick, too," Houdini said. "You just get me an elephant, and I'll make it disappear."

We walked across the street.

"Why don't you make Mr. Morgan disappear instead?" I said. "He's about as big as an elephant."

"Maybe I will," Houdini told me.

Mr. Morgan is a teacher at our school. By mistake he once sat on my lunch. My apple was applesauce.

The Super Big 'N' Super Friendly Supermarket is real big. We didn't find any shopping carts outside, so I knew the store would be crowded. It was. Inside there were long lines of shoppers waiting to pay.

Houdini said, "Maybe someone has finished shopping and can give us his cart."

Most people like to push their carts out to their cars. That way they don't have to carry their grocery bags. We looked at the checkout lines for someone who wasn't buying very much.

A woman in line 1 had only a few things in her cart. We waited.

"You'll have to unload your cart," the clerk told her.

"Oh, yes, of course," the woman said.

She put a pie shell, apples, flour, sugar, cinnamon, cloves, and sour cream on the counter.

"Dutch apple pie?" I asked.

The woman turned and looked at me.

"Are you planning to bake a Dutch apple pie?" I asked.

The woman nodded her head. I think she was surprised that I knew.

"You bought everything in the recipe," I explained. "You know, it's better if you don't cut the apple slices too thin."

"Please," the clerk said. "People are waiting."

The apple pie woman opened her handbag. It was in the cart's baby seat. She took out her purse and opened it.

Suddenly she looked real upset.

"Oh, my goodness. My money is gone!"

The apple pie woman searched through her handbag. She took out some keys, a notepad, a checkbook, and a hairbrush. She dropped everything onto the counter. Then she turned her handbag upside down and shook it. A stick of old gum fell out.

The clerk put the woman's bag of groceries into her shopping cart.

"We're going to have to wait a long time to get her cart," Houdini said.

The people waiting in line started to complain.

"Why would she come here without money?" asked one man.

"She should clean out her handbag at home," said the woman behind him.

The clerk told the woman, "You don't need money. You can pay by check. But you'll have to go to the service desk and fill out some forms."

Now the apple pie woman was looking in the pockets of her coat.

"I'm in a hurry," said the man who was next in line. "Just write a check."

The woman put everything back in her handbag and walked toward the service counter. The clerk pushed her cart out of the way.

Houdini said, "Maybe someone at the express line won't need his cart."

The express—10 items or less—line was line 12. We saw a man put just three items on the counter.

Tissues. Tea. Orange juice. The man must have a cold. I looked at him. Yuck!

His nose was dripping.

"Do you still need your cart?" I asked.

He said he didn't need it. Then he sneezed.

Just as Houdini took the cart we heard an old woman at the next counter say, "What happened to all my money?"

She was looking through the handbag that was in the baby seat of her cart. The woman's green coat looked old and faded.

The clerk told her, "You can pay by check, but you'll have to go to the service desk and fill out some forms."

"I'm not paying by check. And I'm not filling out any forms," said the green coat woman. "I know you steal from me with your high prices. But now you've stolen my money right out of my bag!"

3

M. T. Randal, Super Guard

"She's angry," I whispered to Houdini.

"Shh," he said.

We waited to see what would happen next.

The clerk called over the security guard. He was a fat man with a drooping mustache. The name *M. T. Randal* was sewn on the front of his shirt.

The green coat woman told M. T. Randal, "I know I had money because I just came from the dry cleaners. After I paid them, I had twenty-two dollars left in my wallet. I counted it."

"Maybe you left the money at the cleaners," M. T. Randal said. "Or maybe you're a little mixed up and remember another time."

That made the green coat woman real angry.

"I may be old, but I have not lost my memory," she said. "What I *have* lost is my money. Someone stole it."

M. T. Randal shook his head. "That could not have happened here," he said. "We have cameras hidden throughout the store. I watch the doors and the aisles on my monitors. No one steals anything when Melvin Terrence Randal is on guard."

Melvin Terrence Randal must think he's the world's greatest security guard.

He told the clerk to pack the woman's

groceries. Then he told the woman to come to his office.

M. T. Randal, Super Guard, didn't know that the apple pie woman had lost her money, too. But we did. Suddenly I was sure there was a very busy thief at work in the store. I told that to Houdini.

"Maybe you're right," he told me. "Or maybe M. T. Randal is right. Maybe those two women were just real forgetful."

Well, I still thought that there was a thief at work in the Super Big 'N' Super Friendly Supermarket, and I was going to find him.

"Let's do our shopping," Houdini said. "We have to hurry and get to the meeting."

Houdini pushed the cart toward the vegetable and fruit aisle.

"Excuse me," a man said.

Houdini quickly moved his cart and bumped into a woman reaching for potato chips.

"Why don't you watch where you're going?" the woman asked.

"I'm sorry," Houdini said.

"Let me drive," I told Houdini.

I pushed the cart to the vegetable and fruit aisle. Houdini looked for onions, and I looked for the thief.

The market was real crowded. I wondered how anyone could steal money with so many people around.

Houdini came back with eight onions.

Next we went looking for the plastic spoons and bowls. As we walked, I kept looking for the thief. I thought maybe I'd see him reaching into someone else's pocket.

Suddenly a small boy ran in front of us. I just missed hitting him.

"Didn't I tell you to be careful?" a woman shouted at the boy. She grabbed his hand and pulled him away.

Then a woman with long dark hair walked right into our cart.

"Oops," she said. She was carrying a large box of Toasty Ghosties. She slowly walked around us and put the box of cereal in a cart that was parked nearby. She started to push it away. Then she stopped.

"Hey, this is not my cart," she said real loud. "I didn't buy red tulips."

Love
Toasty Ghosties

She took the Toasty Ghosties out of the cart and hurried off.

You have to be careful when you drive a cart in a supermarket.

I looked both ways, and no one was coming toward us.

"There should be traffic lights here," I said to Houdini as I slowly pushed our cart.

We found the plastic spoons and bowls. Houdini chose purple spoons and orange bowls. He's very smart, but he's terrible with colors.

I told him that. He said, "I'm just ahead of my time. You'll see. In a few years everyone will be wearing purple and orange together."

I doubt it.

We went to the ice cream freezer. I took the last container of vanilla, chocolate, and strawberry.

I looked at my list. We had everything.

"Well, that's it," I said. "Now we can get in line to check out."

Houdini shook his head. "I need one more thing."

I looked at my list again. Then I looked at the things in our cart. I wondered what we still needed.

Houdini reached for the cart.

"Now, be careful," I told him. "Look both ways before crossing an aisle. Don't get too close to the cart in front of you. Don't drive too fast."

I followed Houdini to the baking aisle. He took a jar of chocolate syrup from the shelf and looked at the price. "I can't afford to buy one for everyone in the club," he said. "We'll have to share."

Houdini put four jars into our cart.

Of course! Houdini didn't really change

an onion into a jar of chocolate syrup! Somehow he made a switch.

We went to the express checkout line. We waited for our turn to pay.

"Did you make the switch in the tube?" I asked.

Houdini didn't answer.

"You couldn't have. I saw the tube and it was empty."

Houdini smiled. It wasn't one of his real big magic show smiles. I only saw his front teeth.

"Was there a jar of chocolate sauce inside the onion?" I asked.

He just looked straight ahead.

"Please, tell me how you did it."

"I will," Houdini promised. "I'll tell you at the meeting."

The man at the front of our line paid

for his things. We moved two steps closer to the checkout counter.

The woman just ahead of us unloaded her cart. She was buying milk, Toasty Ghosties, juice, and bread. Then she took her handbag from the baby seat.

She was the Toasty Ghosty woman we had seen earlier. The woman who had lost her cart.

She took her wallet out, opened it, and said, "What happened to my money?"

I whispered to Houdini, "She's the third person to lose money."

"Did you search all the pockets of your handbag?" the clerk asked.

"I have to think about this," Houdini mumbled. He was talking to himself. He does that sometimes.

The Toasty Ghosty woman looked

through her handbag. It had lots of pockets. She was checking them all.

Houdini whispered to me, "All three of the people who lost money were women."

The Toasty Ghosty woman was still looking through her handbag.

"Aha!" Houdini said real loud.

People waiting on other lines turned to look at him.

He was excited and spoke very fast. "All three women had handbags. They all kept their handbags in their carts.

"You can stop looking," he told the Toasty Ghosty woman. "Your money is gone. It was stolen. There's a shopping cart thief in this store. She's clever, but so am I. I know just how she works."

4
It's a Switch

The clerk and the Toasty Ghosty woman just looked at Houdini.

"My name is Houdini Foster," he said. "I'm a magician. And it's a switch, just like I do with my Onion Sundae Trick."

"What's happening on Sunday?" the woman asked.

"You left your handbag in the cart," Houdini went on. "Someone switched carts with you and then stole your money."

"Linguini Foster may be right," the Toasty Ghosty woman told the clerk.

"While I was shopping, someone did take my cart. I thought it was a mistake."

"My name is not Linguini. It's Houdini. And did you see who switched carts with you?"

"No," the Toasty Ghosty woman said. "I found my cart in the next aisle, by the tomato sauce cans. My handbag was just where I left it, in the seat."

The clerk called M. T. Randal. The Toasty Ghosty woman told him about her missing money. Houdini told M. T. Randal that the money was stolen.

"Nothing was taken here," said M. T. Randal, Super Guard. "Nothing was stolen. That never happens when I'm on guard."

He told the woman, "We can talk in my office. Meanwhile, you can fill out some forms, and write a check for the groceries."

The Toasty Ghosty woman walked away with M. T. Randal. The clerk packed her groceries and put them under the counter.

We still had not unloaded our cart.

"We have evidence of a crime," said Houdini. "Now we must search for clues."

"Are you planning to pay for your things or play detective?" asked a woman on line behind us. "I'm in a hurry."

Houdini turned to the woman and smiled. It was one of his real big magic show smiles. "I'm going to play detective," he said. "My name is Detective Houdini. I'd like to ask you some questions. Where were you at ten o'clock this morning? Is Herkemeyer your real name?"

"I have no time for your games, and my name is *not* Herkemeyer," she told Houdini. "I'm in a hurry."

"Let's go," I whispered.

"I'm sorry," I said to the woman. "He doesn't mean to be rude."

I pushed the cart to the fresh flowers aisle. It wasn't crowded there.

"I know exactly how the thief works," Houdini told me. "She looks for women who keep their handbags in the baby seat. She waits until one of them leaves her cart. Then she switches carts. She leaves her own cart and pushes the stolen cart to another aisle. Then she takes the money."

"How do you know the thief is a woman?" I asked.

Houdini explained, "That way, when she looks through the stolen handbag, everyone thinks it's hers."

We began looking for the thief in the

fresh flowers aisle. A woman was there with her small son.

"These are daisies," she said. "The name comes from the words *day's eyes* because these flowers look like eyes. They open during the day and close at night."

"Mom, I don't want to hear about flowers," the boy said. "I want to find the chocolate doughnuts."

That woman wasn't the thief. A thief wouldn't take her son along.

We went to the soap aisle. A woman was reading the side of a detergent box. Then she threw it into her cart and went on shopping. The other shoppers were dropping things into their carts, too. None of them did anything suspicious.

I told Houdini, "We're not going to find

the shopping cart thief. Everyone here is really shopping."

"Detectives must be patient," he said. "Sometimes they have to search for hours, even days, before they find the smallest clue."

I couldn't search for days. I had to be home in time for supper.

We went to the household cleaners aisle. The only things we found there were household cleaners.

Then we went to the soda and snacks aisle. A young woman there was turning over bags of pretzel sticks. She saw me watching.

"I'm looking for one without too many broken pieces," she explained.

A teenage boy was shaking cans of roasted peanuts.

"How do you like it?" he asked. "I'm making peanut can music."

"It's very nice," I told him. But it wasn't. To me it sounded more like peanut can *noise.*

We went to the tomato sauce and pasta aisle.

Houdini whispered, "Do you remember what the Toasty Ghosty woman said? She found her cart near the tomato sauce cans. That means the thief was here before. Maybe she's still here."

The shoppers there were all in a hurry. They found what they wanted, put it in their carts, and moved on.

Then I saw a woman who was pushing her cart very slowly through the aisle. She was looking at a piece of paper. Not at the cans and boxes on the shelves.

We watched her for a while. I saw her look a few times at the other shoppers and their carts.

"Houdini," I whispered. "Look at her. She's not shopping. She's just pretending."

She went to the end of the aisle. Then she turned around and came toward us.

The woman was young. She was wearing a dark blue jogging suit and sneakers. Those are great clothes for robbing someone and then running away.

Houdini turned our cart around and whispered to me, "You see. I was right. I am a great detective. I told you we would find the thief in the tomato sauce aisle. And we did."

5

Green Noodles

Houdini whispered, "Let's watch her. Maybe we'll catch her making a switch. But we have to be careful. She's a thief. She may be dangerous."

Houdini stopped. He took a box of spinach noodles off the shelf and gave it to me.

"Should we buy these?" he asked in a loud voice.

"They're green," I said. "I don't eat green things."

The jogging suit woman walked past us.

"I like white noodles," I said.

"I'm just pretending to be shopping," Houdini whispered.

Then he put his finger to his lips. He wanted me to be quiet. He pointed at the woman. She reached the end of our aisle and turned right.

"Let's follow her," Houdini whispered.

He pushed the cart ahead and left me there with the green noodles. I put the box back on the shelf and caught up with Houdini.

The jogging suit woman was in the cereal and dried fruit aisle. She still wasn't putting anything in her cart.

At the end of the aisle, she turned around and came toward us. Houdini reached for a giant box of pitted prunes.

"Do we need these?" he asked real loud.

I said, "I hope not."

Houdini put the box in our cart.

I told him, "If we eat all those prunes, we'll get a giant case of diarrhea."

Houdini put his finger to his lips again. The woman was getting closer.

Houdini reached for a box of raisins.

The jogging suit woman walked past us and turned right at the end of the aisle.

Houdini handed me the raisins. "Put these back, and the prunes, too. I'll follow her."

I put the raisins back on the shelf. I reached into the cart for the prunes and I saw the ice cream. I felt the package. It was getting soft. I had to put it back in the freezer before it melted.

I pushed the cart to the frozen foods aisle. The only ice cream flavors left were butter pecan and blueberry swirl.

Chocolate syrup on blueberry swirl! Yuck!

I put our vanilla, chocolate, and strawberry at the bottom of the freezer. I covered it with two butter pecans. I hoped no one else would find it.

Just then I saw a cart with a handbag in the baby seat. No one was standing nearby. This was a perfect chance for the shopping cart thief to strike again.

I waited and watched. Then a short white-haired woman came up to the cart and pushed it away. She didn't look like a thief. But sometimes looks can fool you. I followed the woman.

She walked toward a large display of paper towels and mops. The woman stopped. She opened the handbag.

This is it, I thought. She's about to steal the money.

She took out some yellow and purple papers.

I moved a few steps closer.

It wasn't money. She was holding coupons. She wasn't the thief.

The woman put the coupons away. She started to take a roll of paper towels from the middle of the display.

"Don't!" I shouted. The tower of towels was about to fall.

I ran up and pushed the roll back in.

"I can't reach the top," she said.

I couldn't either.

I took a mop. I used the long handle to knock off a roll of towels from the top of the tower. I caught it. I'm good at catching things.

"Thank you," she said.

I looked around for Houdini. I found him back in the noodle aisle. He was still following the jogging suit woman.

"She keeps looking around," Houdini whispered.

We watched her walk up and down the noodle aisle. She looked around. Then she walked away from her cart. She was walking faster now. At first I thought she was walking toward us. But she wasn't. There was a cart with no one standing nearby. That's where the woman was headed.

"This is it," Houdini whispered. "She's about to make a switch."

6

Quick! Grab a Box!

"We can't get too close," Houdini told me. "We don't want to scare her off."

Houdini took a box off the shelf. "Look at this picture," he said. "Noodles in the shapes of vegetables. Onions. Celery. Wow!"

I said, "Yuck! I wouldn't eat an onion or anything that looks like an onion."

The jogging suit woman was walking quickly now. She walked right past us.

Houdini was right. I was sure of it. This woman was about to make a switch.

We kept watching her. She got to the

end of the noodle aisle. She turned around and walked toward us.

Did the jogging suit woman know that we suspected her?

Houdini said, "Quick! Grab a box!"

We each took a box of noodles off the shelf and threw them into our cart.

The woman walked past us. She took her handbag from the baby seat of her cart and walked by us again. We followed her to the front of the store, to the service desk.

Houdini and I got close. We stood between a tall tower of tuna fish cans and a small tower of pickle jars. We each took a can and pretended to read the labels. And we listened.

"I've been looking all over for Dragon Tail Noodles. They're on sale, and I can't find them anywhere."

SALE

"Aisle seven, near the front," the woman at the service desk said.

The jogging suit woman walked away.

She wasn't looking for a handbag to steal. She was looking for noodles. We were lousy detectives.

I put my tuna fish can back.

"We're wasting our time," I said to Houdini. "While we were following her, the real thief probably stole again. She might even have left the store. And someone might have found our vanilla, chocolate, and strawberry ice cream."

Houdini stared at me. I looked into his deep dark brown eyes.

"I buried it under two butter pecans," I told him.

Houdini didn't answer. I waved my hand in front of him. He didn't even blink. Houdini was thinking. He does that sometimes.

He looked weird. His eyes were wide open. His mouth was open, too. And he was holding a can of tuna fish.

"We missed it," he said.

"We missed what?"

"We missed the big clue. You said it yourself. You said we were watching the jogging suit woman, and that's where we made our mistake. We were watching the wrong thing."

After he does a trick, Houdini always tells me, *You were watching the wrong thing. Never look at the magician. Watch his props.*

"But now I know what to look for!" said Houdini. "Now I know how to find the shopping cart thief!"

7

Catching Thieves Is My Job

"We were looking for the thief," Houdini said. "And that was a mistake. We should have been looking for the thief's cart."

"That's silly," I said. "We want to catch a thief. Not a cart."

Houdini shook his head.

"The people who were robbed never saw the thief. But they did see her cart. She left it in place of the one she took. Remember what the Toasty Ghosty woman said when she looked into the wrong cart? She said she *didn't buy red tulips.* We have to look for a cart with red tulips inside. When we find it, we'll find the thief."

I looked at my watch. We were already late for the meeting.

"We can't keep chasing this thief," I said. "Let's tell M. T. Randal what we know. He can catch the thief and we can go to Dana's."

"No," Houdini said.

"Yes," I told him.

I stamped my foot down to let him know I meant it.

Crunch!

Someone had spilled potato chips on the floor. The Super Big 'N' Super Friendly Supermarket wasn't super clean.

I pushed the cart to M. T. Randal's office. He was sitting at his desk, eating a salad. French dressing was dripping from his mustache. This Super Guard was super sloppy.

M. T. Randal looked up and saw us.

"What do you want?" he asked.

"I can help you," Houdini said.

M. T. Randal grunted. Then he stuck the fork in a tomato slice. He dipped it in some dressing and ate the tomato.

Houdini said, "I know how to find the thief."

M. T. Randal pointed the fork at us and said, "There is no thief. And even if there were, I wouldn't need a little boy's help to find him."

French dressing dripped from the fork and onto his desk.

"I'm not an ordinary boy," Houdini told M. T. Randal. "I'm almost a genius. I'm a magician, too."

He put his hand near my ear and a penny fell out.

Then he made a fist with his other hand. He dropped the penny in. When he opened his fist, the penny was gone.

M. T. Randal looked at me.

"I'm not a genius or a magician," I told him. "I'm just an ordinary girl."

M. T. Randal grunted again.

"Maybe you're right," Houdini said. "Maybe there is no thief. But don't you want to know for sure?"

M. T. Randal put down his fork.

"OK," he said. "If there is a thief, where is he?"

"She," I said.

Houdini told M. T. Randal about the cart switch trick and the red tulips.

"Thank you," M. T. Randal said. "Now run along, children. Catching thieves is my job. I'll watch for the cart and the thief on my monitors."

There were about ten small TVs on the wall above his desk. Each screen showed a different part of the store.

M. T. Randal warned us, "Now, don't you look for the thief. Thieves can be dangerous."

Houdini smiled. Then, as soon as we were out of the office, he whispered to me, "I'll find her."

8
Then We Saw Red Tulips

"But it may be dangerous," I said. "And we're already late for the meeting."

I don't think Houdini even heard me.

He said, "We'll look for a cart with red tulips inside."

"We can look," I said. "But just for a few minutes."

I pushed our cart. I was real careful. I didn't want to bump into anyone.

We looked as we walked. We didn't look at the people. We looked at what they had in their carts.

I played a game. First I looked at the groceries. Then I guessed what the person buying them was like.

I saw one cart filled with cookies, peanuts, and potato chips. I guessed that the person pushing the cart was fat. I was right.

Another cart had diapers, baby food, and milk. I guessed that the person pushing the cart had a baby. I was right again. There was a baby sitting in the baby seat.

Near the noodle aisle Houdini pointed to a camera hanging from the ceiling. "I think we're on one of M. T. Randal's TVs," he whispered.

We went slowly from one aisle to the next. We looked in every cart we passed.

We saw lots of carts with something red inside. But when we got closer we saw that they weren't tulips. All kinds of cereals, noodles, pretzels, and laundry soaps come in red boxes.

Then we saw red tulips.

The cart was near the meats. No one was pushing it, or even standing nearby.

I whispered to Houdini, "Maybe she just made a switch."

He put his finger to his lips. He wanted me to be quiet.

We waited.

"Maybe she left the store," I whispered.

We waited some more.

Finally a woman walked up to the cart. She was wearing a dark blue jacket, black slacks, and sneakers.

We followed her as she slowly pushed the cart. Maybe she would suddenly realize it wasn't hers. Maybe this woman's money had just been stolen. But she just kept pushing the cart and looking.

Then, when we were only a few steps behind her, she turned and looked at me. I looked down. I waited. Then I looked up. She was still looking at me.

Finally the red tulip woman turned and started to walk away.

"Let's go," I whispered to Houdini.

"No," he told me. "I think we found her."

Houdini is smart. He's almost a genius. But then he did something that wasn't smart at all.

He looked up until he found one of M. T. Randal's hidden cameras.

Then Houdini began waving wildly.

"What are you doing?" I asked.

"I'm signaling to M. T. Randal," he whispered. "I found the thief. Now he has to arrest her."

A woman holding a large bag of popcorn thought Houdini was waving to her. She waved back.

"You look silly," I whispered.

An old man holding a loaf of bread thought Houdini was waving to him. The man waved the bread at Houdini.

The red tulip woman turned left at the end of the snack aisle. As she turned, she looked at me again. Then she saw Houdini waving.

She stared at him for a moment. A lot of people were staring. He looked real strange, waving to the ceiling.

Then the red tulip woman looked up. She saw the hidden camera.

She started to run.

9
Stop! Thief!

Houdini ran after her yelling, "Stop! Thief!"

Of course, the woman didn't stop.

She kicked the paper towel tower, and rolls of towels tumbled down. Houdini tripped over a roll and fell. I didn't. I jumped over one rolling towel roll after another. Like a horse in one of those fence-jumping races.

The woman turned and saw me.

She kicked the tower of tuna fish cans and the pickle jar tower next to it. Tuna

cans rolled toward the checkout counters and down the aisles. Jars of pickles fell and broke.

"Breakage in aisle three. Breakage in aisle three," someone said over the store loudspeakers.

I stopped running. I didn't want to trip over a tuna can or slip in pickle juice.

I walked carefully to the front door of the store. M. T. Randal was standing there, holding on to the shopping cart thief.

"I caught her," he said. "She's not getting away from me."

People on their way into the store stopped to look.

Houdini and a woman wearing a light gray smock came running. The words *G. Nunez, Store Manager* were sewn onto the front of her smock.

"Call the police," M. T. Randal told G. Nunez. "This woman is a thief, and I caught her."

He wouldn't have caught the thief without our help. That's for sure.

G. Nunez was carrying a walkie-talkie. She spoke into it.

"Sylvia, call the police. Tell them to come right away. We caught a thief."

M. T. Randal said, "She's been switching carts and stealing people's money. I caught her just as she was leaving."

Super Guard M. T. Randal forgot that Houdini and I had helped.

The thief had her head down.

"Tell your friends about Melvin Terrence Randal," Super Guard told the thief. "Tell them that if they try stealing here, I'll catch them. I'll catch them all."

"*You'll* catch them!" Houdini said. He was almost shouting. "I was the one who discovered the thefts. I was the one who found her."

"*We* found her," I said.

Houdini, the almost genius, and M. T. Randal, Super Guard, are a lot alike that way. They both like to take *all* the credit.

We heard sirens. We saw flashing lights. Then two police cars came speeding into the parking lot.

M. T. Randal and G. Nunez spoke to the police. The officers put the woman in the backseat of one of the cars and drove off.

Then G. Nunez asked M. T. Randal, "Did these children discover the thefts?"

M. T. Randal nodded.

"Did they help you catch that woman?"

M. T. Randal nodded again.

"Well, then," G. Nunez said to us. "You deserve a reward."

She told us our groceries would be a gift from the Super Big 'N' Super Friendly Supermarket.

We walked around the tuna fish cans, broken pickle jars, and paper towel rolls. We put back the noodles. Then we went to the ice cream freezer. Our vanilla, chocolate, and strawberry was still there, under a container of butter pecan.

We told G. Nunez our names and telephone numbers. "There may be a news story about this," she said. "And if there is, I want you to be in it."

We left the store and walked through the parking lot. When we got to the corner, Houdini stopped.

"Well, I'm glad that's over," he said. "I couldn't wait to get out of there. The whole place smelled of pickles."

10
The Great Houdini

Dana was on her front porch, waiting for us.

"You're late," she said.

"I'm worth waiting for," Houdini told her as he walked past. "I have a great trick to show you."

Dana and I followed him down to the basement. There was a table and chairs set up. Everyone was there. Jordan, Melissa, Rachel, Daniel, Maria, and Tony.

Houdini went into the small storage room. While he was in there, I told everyone about the thief we had caught.

"Nice going," Dana said.

Melissa said, "It must have been scary."

Then Houdini came out of the storage room. He was wearing his cape and his big magic show smile. He was carrying his magic wand, an onion, a dish of vanilla, chocolate, and strawberry ice cream, and the red tube.

"Follow me, the Great Houdini," he said, "for a taste of some delicious magic."

He sat behind the table. We all sat on the other side of the table and waited.

"Good afternoon, ladies and gentlemen," he called out to us. "I, the Great Houdini, am about to mystify and amaze you."

He smiled.

"My cousin Janet Perry is about to eat an onion sundae."

Houdini looked at me.

I looked at him.

"Do you want to eat an onion sundae?" he asked me.

I told him, "Of course not."

"Aha!" Houdini shouted. "My cousin says she doesn't like onions. I guess I'll have to change this onion into something she does like."

Houdini gave his big magic show smile. I saw tonsils.

"*Ala-kazam*, I am great. Yes, I am," he said. And he did his Onion Sundae Trick.

This time I watched his hands, the onion, and the red paper tube very carefully. Suddenly, I got it!

"How did you do that?" Jordan asked.

"I, the Great Houdini, will teach you," answered Houdini.

He swirled his cape and began to explain.

Meanwhile, I took the dish of vanilla, chocolate, and strawberry ice cream from the table. I poured lots of chocolate syrup over the top.

Yum!

The Onion Sundae Trick

by Bob Friedhoffer

NOTE: This trick is to be performed while seated at a table.

EFFECT:

An onion changes into a jar of chocolate sauce.

PROPS:

Piece of heavy construction paper, approximately 8" x 10"

Rubber band

A small jar or can of chocolate sauce

A small onion
(The onion should be the same diameter as the jar of chocolate sauce.)

Ice cream, scoop, bowls, and spoons

PREPARATION:

• Roll the construction paper into a 10-inch-long tube. The tube should be wide enough to hold the jar of chocolate sauce.

• Place the rubber band around the tube, to prevent the tube from unrolling.

• Place the jar of chocolate sauce into the tube.

• Stand the tube, on end, about 8 inches to your left.

• Place the onion 6 inches from the edge of the table, directly in front of you.

The sundae ingredients are on the table, but out of the way.

ROUTINE AND PATTER:

"Let's have ice cream sundaes. We'll make it my favorite. Onion sundaes!"

• Pick up the onion and show it to your friends. At least one of them should say, "Yuck!" or something like that, unless you have very strange friends.

"Oh, you don't want an onion sundae? What would you like? Maybe a chocolate sundae?"

At least one person will say, "Yes!"

"Then watch carefully as I turn this onion into chocolate sauce."

• Pick up the onion with your left hand, and make mysterious motions over it with your right hand, or with a magic wand. Then say some magic words, such as "abracadabra."

• Drop the onion into the tube so it falls onto the jar of chocolate sauce.

• With your right hand, squeeze the tube and the onion gently. Pick the tube straight up with your right hand. If you have done this properly, the chocolate sauce is now in sight, and the onion is hidden inside of the tube.

"The magic has worked. I have changed the onion into chocolate sauce."

• As you say this, pick up the chocolate sauce with your left hand. Bring the right hand and tube to the edge of the table, directly above your lap. As the tube reaches the edge of the table, loosen your grip on the onion, allowing it to fall into your lap. You are still holding on to the tube. As soon as the onion is in your lap, gently drop the tube onto the table.

"Now let's have a sundae!"

Open up the chocolate sauce, scoop out the ice cream, make a bunch of sundaes, and enjoy yourselves.

NOTE: When you want to stand up, drop your hand into your lap, pick up the onion, and, as you rise from the chair, slip the onion into your pocket.

You can switch any two items this way as long as they both fit into the tube. An apple for an orange, a rubber ball for a tomato, an apple for a jar of applesauce, or anything else that you can think of!

Don't miss the next Houdini Club Magic Mystery!

I was in big trouble.

"I need your help," I told Houdini. "It was my job to take care of Alfred. And now he's gone."

"I, the Great Houdini, will help you find him."

Houdini always tells me how great he is.

If he finds Alfred, I'll believe it.

From *Wacky Jacks*
(A Houdini Club Magic Mystery)
by David A. Adler

About the Authors

DAVID ADLER loves magic, but sometimes his tricks work a little too well. He made his watch disappear once—and never found it.

David lives in Woodmere, New York, with his wife, a psychologist, and their three sons, none of whom is named Herman. David has written many books for children, including the acclaimed *Cam Jansen* series.

BOB FRIEDHOFFER, known as the "Madman of Magic," created the Onion Sundae Trick. Bob has been a magician for over fifteen years and has even performed at the White House. He currently lives and works in New York City.